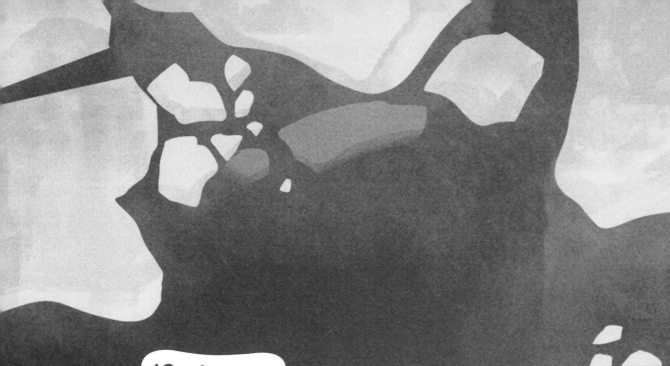

10 Minute Classics

Good books are some of the greatest treasures in the world. They can take you to incredible places and on fantastic adventures. So sit back with a **10 MINUTE CLASSIC** and indulge a lifelong love for reading.

We cannot, however, guarantee your 10 minute break won't turn into 15, 20, or 30 minutes, as these FUN stories and engaging pictures will have you turning the pages AGAIN and AGAIN!

Designed by Flowerpot Press
in Franklin, TN.
www.FlowerpotPress.com
Designer: Stephanie Meyers
Editor: Katrine Crow
DJS-0912-0160
ISBN: 978-1-4867-1200-7
Made in China/Fabriqué en Chine

AUG 19 2017

Moby Dick

Herman Melville

Retold by
Philip Edwards

Illustrated by
Adam Horsepool

10 Minute
Classics

Call me Ishmael. This is my story. It is a story that happened some years ago and that took me well out into the world. I had little to my name and little to lose, and the call of the open waters was tugging at my soul. I was destined for a world of water, whales, and wild adventure...

My adventure began in a port town filled with men of the sea. It was there I met Queequeg, a harpooner from the South Seas, and we soon became fine friends. Queequeg was from a far-off island where his father was a king. Despite his noble ways and the promise of one day being king himself, Queequeg's longing to see and learn about the world had sent him on a journey that permanently pulled him from his homeland. We were joined together in the desire to continue that journey and soon after meeting, we headed for the island of Nantucket. There we would find a ship and set our sights on the world beyond.

In Nantucket, Queequeg and I settled on the *Pequod*, a whaling ship owned by two rich men and captained by the mysterious Captain Ahab. Despite ominous warnings, Queequeg and I stayed committed to the *Pequod*, its owners, and its curious captain.

The *Pequod* set sail on a cold winter's day, Christmas no less! As we journeyed to sea, I was reminded of just how noble our adventure was. Whaling is a necessary part of our world, serving industry and kings alike, and we were one of the chosen few commissioned to search for these beasts of the open waters.

I quickly came to know my many shipmates: Flask, Tashtego, Stubb, Starbuck, Daggoo, Pip, and many others. They were a fine and varied collection of men from the world over, but none compared to the captain himself.

When Captain Ahab finally joined us on deck, his unique appearance struck me immediately. With a leg carved from whalebone and a lightning strike of a scar down his face, he was a strong, determined figure with an air of turmoil. He quickly took full command of ship and crew and the work of the *Pequod* began. Captain Ahab made it clear that our real work was not just hunting whales; we were hunting a specific whale—the great white whale they called Moby Dick!

Moby Dick was a whale of legend. Seamen the world over told of the great white whale and his mystical abilities. He was rumored to be immortal and capable of appearing in many places at once. Moby Dick was uncatchable. Even Captain Ahab had failed in his last attempt to land Moby Dick, losing his leg in the process. Perhaps it was that defeat that drove our captain so fiercely. Although we hunted and caught other whales on our journey, to Captain Ahab, there was only one real prize and one true destiny for ship and crew.

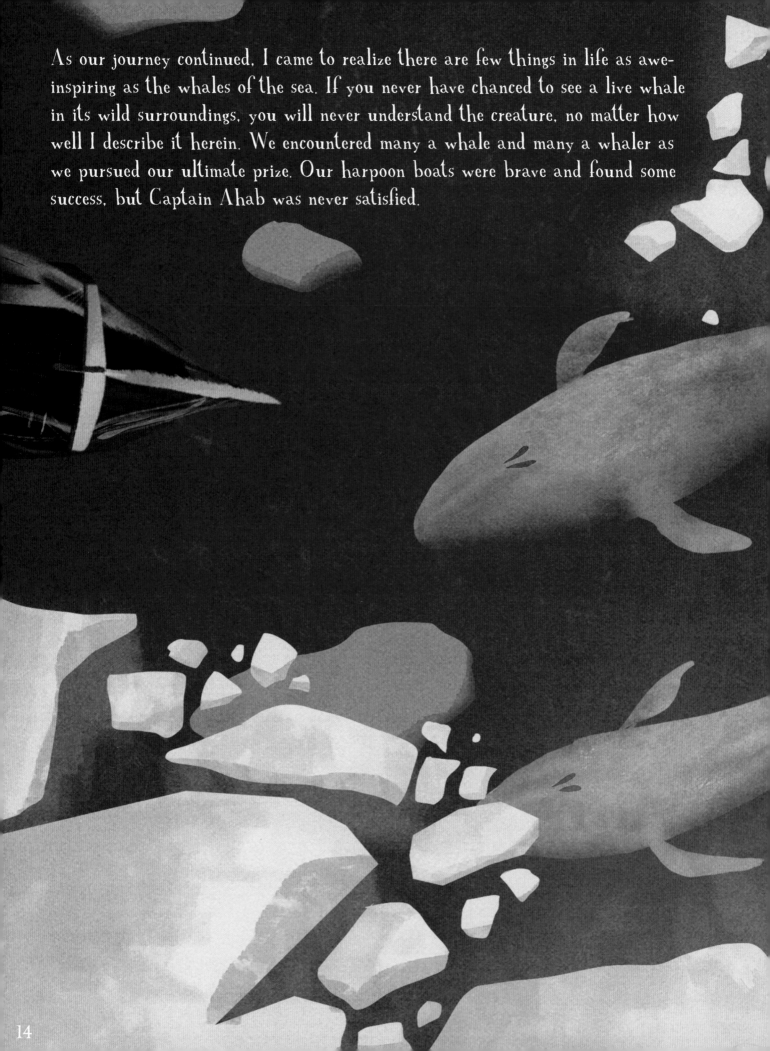

As our journey continued, I came to realize there are few things in life as awe-inspiring as the whales of the sea. If you never have chanced to see a live whale in its wild surroundings, you will never understand the creature, no matter how well I describe it herein. We encountered many a whale and many a whaler as we pursued our ultimate prize. Our harpoon boats were brave and found some success, but Captain Ahab was never satisfied.

As we continued our search for Moby Dick we met sailors along the way who had already encountered our prey. Alas, they had all been left disappointed, and some worse. Yet all this merely fueled our captain, who continued to make preparations for what he felt was his destiny. He had the ship's carpenter carve him a new, studier leg and had the ship's blacksmith forge him a special harpoon. Captain Ahab's singular focus had many aboard questioning his soundness, as well as our own fates. (At one point my dear friend Queequeg even commissioned a casket, fearing he would die at sea.)

As we made our way toward
the equator, Captain Ahab
began to feel as though we were
closing in on our target. He was soon
proven prescient* when we came upon
another whaler, the *Rachel*. The captain of
the *Rachel* tried to dissuade us from our quest
for the great white whale, as his son had been lost
during their own attempts to land Moby Dick.

The captain was hoping for our assistance in searching for his lost son. Rather than stirring sympathy in Captain Ahab, the story of the captain's son only made Captain Ahab more determined to claim his prize. Shortly thereafter, we parted ways.

*Prescient means showing knowledge of events before they happen.

With news that we were close, all focus was firmly on the mission. The crew watched day and night for the elusive beast, but none more intently than our captain. Starbuck began to worry about the captain and with nerves on edge, he tried to reason with him. He explained that our search may in fact be too perilous. But even with Starbuck's sound reasoning, Captain Ahab could not be deterred—the *Pequod* wasn't to stop until we found Moby Dick!

As fate would have it, it was Captain Ahab himself who first spotted Moby Dick...in fact he was the first to SMELL Moby Dick! He thrust his nose in the air like a dog and immediately set us on course for the great white whale. He insisted we hoist him up the masthead as we made our pursuit. Before he had even reached the top, he let out a loud cry, "There she blows! There she blows! A hump like a snow-hill! It's Moby Dick!" The whole crew sprung into action. Our harpoon boats were hastily launched. This was it!!

But this was not it. Today was not to be our day. Rather than us claiming the prize of Moby Dick, Moby Dick claimed a prize of his own—our captain's harpoon boat. It was a bitter battle and we were lucky to have saved our captain and ourselves.

However, this wasn't the end. Sure enough, the next day found us once again locked in a deadly fight as we set our sights on Moby Dick.

Caught up in the captain's passion and our residual anger from the previous day, we worked as one in the hunt. But as with the day before, it was the great whale who would triumph, claiming both boats and crew. Still, our determined Captain Ahab pressed on.

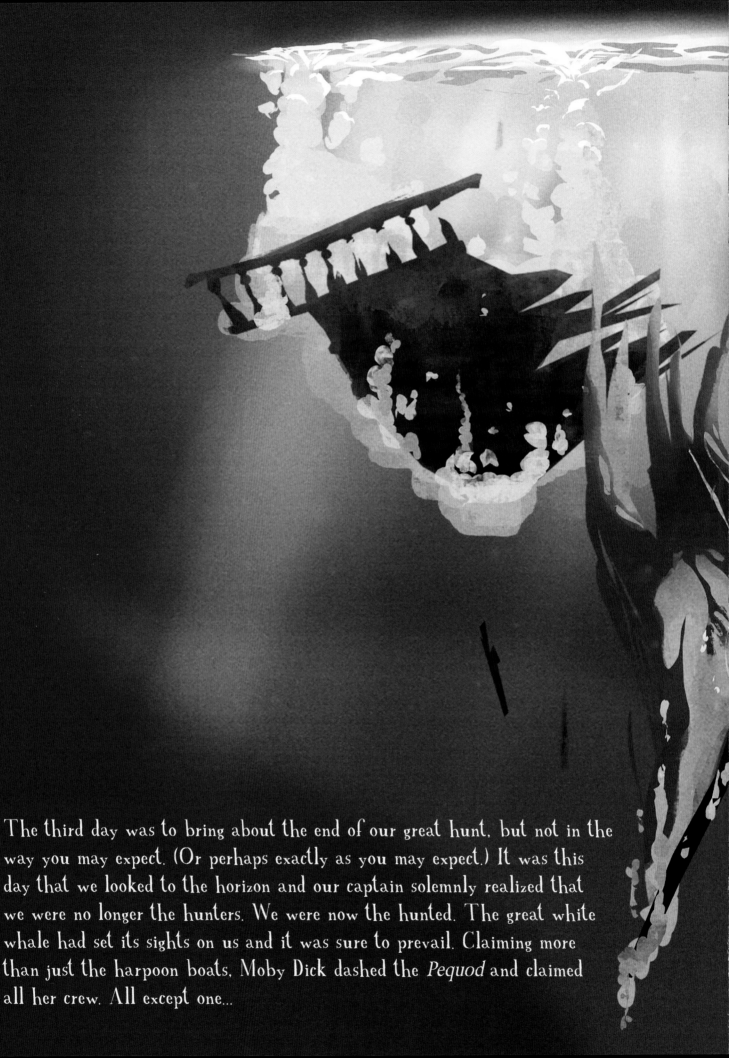

The third day was to bring about the end of our great hunt, but not in the way you may expect. (Or perhaps exactly as you may expect.) It was this day that we looked to the horizon and our captain solemnly realized that we were no longer the hunters. We were now the hunted. The great white whale had set its sights on us and it was sure to prevail. Claiming more than just the harpoon boats, Moby Dick dashed the *Pequod* and claimed all her crew. All except one...

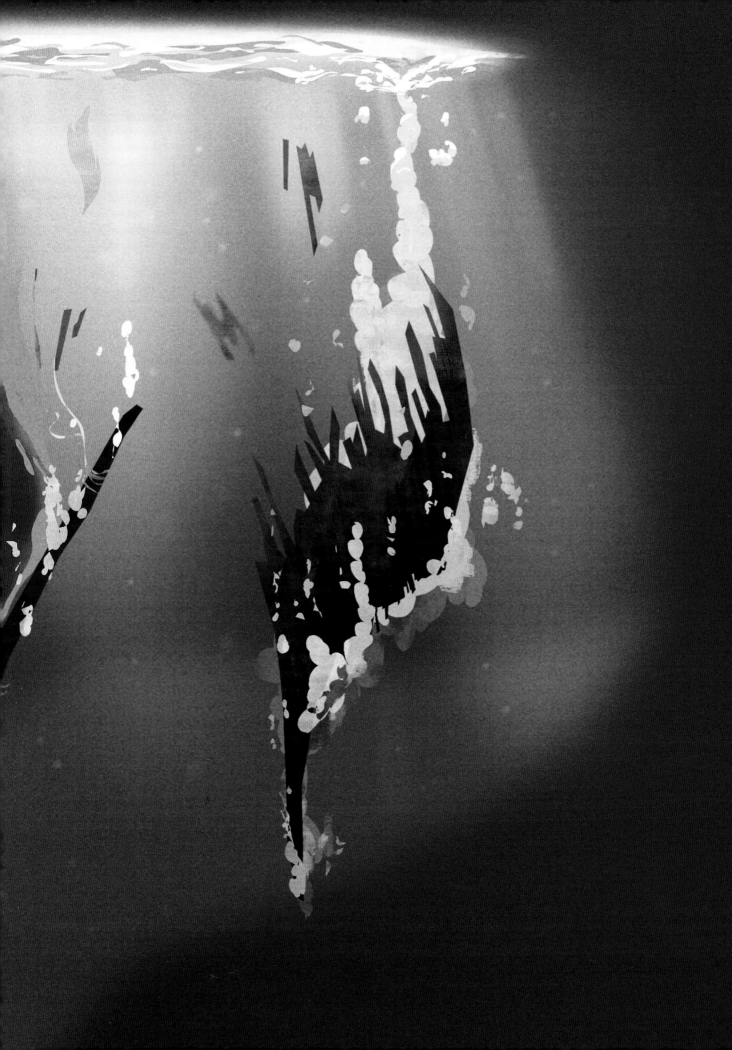

With the *Pequod* destroyed and the boats and crew lost, there was nothing but a few wooden remains and me alone floating at sea. I came upon a lifesaver in the shape of a coffin. It was none other than the coffin Queequeg had commissioned earlier in our journey. Rather than carrying him to his final resting place, it carried me to safety. I floated out on the desolate blue seas for two days until the *Rachel* found this lost sailor and brought him home.

I believe to this day that Moby Dick intentionally left a single witness to tell the tale of our mighty battle...

And now I have.